# STORIES OF YOUNG LIFE

## TWO SHORT STORIES



SHREYA SHOKEEN

# Contents

# Author's Note:

**These stories I share with you are a glimpse of a journey my elder sister has embarked upon as I kept on encouraging her from the sidelines and from which I learned a lot. I wish you well for your future endowers my dear sister. I thank my English teachers to encourage me to write as well as the library teachers to introduce me to the world of reading other authors who became my inspiration and my parents for their constant support and guidance. my dear readers, I hope you enjoy this short compilation of two stories to the fullest. Without further delay let's get started...**

# 1

# Exams are over!!!

The relief, of finishing your final exams. As you lament over what you will do in the coming days and hold about you an atmosphere of celebration!

# Exams are over!!!

It was a day like any other day, or so it seemed. Having holidays after exams is the best. Yesterday was my science exam and surprising enough it was nerve recking. I mean, like up until eighth standard science was science. But, suddenly in ninth, it was physics, chemistry, and biology and the escalation of the level of difficulty was like the scene where a person is climbing a staircase one elevation at a time and suddenly leaping four steps and climbing. If you can imagine that Great!! You understand a bit of my pain. If not! Then you are mean and that's the period.

Has it ever happened to you that time suddenly slows down when you are in the evaluation room? Doing your paper with full concentration and when you reach the final question, with your hand paining to the point that you want to throw down the pen you hold. The examiner suddenly says "TIMES UP!! Give up your answer sheets".

Thankfully, I was in the back row, so I had time until my answer sheet was collected. So, I did the final question, not having time to revise. As soon as I put the full stop on the paper the overbearing shadow of the examiner loomed over me. The feeling I felt was the same as the time my sister caught me eating chocolate at midnight as she woke up to drink water. And I was like busted!! I am going to hear it from mom in the morning. But strangely enough, sis joined me, and it was the bonding feeling of partners in crime. And that secret was ours and only ours. Oh! How brilliant it was, I still have a tear of joy remembering that and our parents didn't find out where that chocolate bar went.

I went off-topic, didn't I? Moving on, it was a sixty-mark question paper and the answer sheet given to us had four sheets, and on the first sheet, details were asked. And right next to it, a box was given saying a number of continuation sheets used. If you have guessed it right then BRAVO!! A thread is also given along with the paper if you require extra sheets. Then you can tag them up along with the main sheet. As I had taken six extra sheets, I still had to tie them all up. But the examiner was standing right there!! And thoughts such as "No! my paper is canceled" OR "Only my main sheet would be submitted? and the rest of the hard work will go down the drain!" etc. were running here and there. Thankfully and surprisingly, the examiner put down the sheets he had collected right next to my desk and organized my answer sheets, and tied them up. Not only that afterward Sir also even gave me a pat on the back and said "Good job!! Well, Done!!" With such a kind smile and with that the scary image of the invigilator shattered and became like a big fuzzy bear who seems scary, but quite approachable.

My teachers are the best, aren't they? I wanted to throw away the pen and tear the question paper and light the question paper on fire shouting with relief "Burn in hell". With a mad laugh following the action. But I can't just do that in the exam room, so I just placed my stationary gracefully in the pouch and started to wait to be dispersed which was only in the following two minutes.

After that, we were dispersed. But, were not yet allowed to go out of the school gate as twelfth-grade seniors were still in the process of giving their exams on the fourth floor of the school building. My examination room was on the ground floor, so reaching the basketball court was not that hard. All I had to do was make my way through the hallways after picking up my bag which is right outside the room near the door. I was beyond glad that no one stomped on my bag as the students in the examination rooms alongside ours too poured out into the corridors creating a stampede.

With the pouch attached to the clipboard by clipping, one corner of the pouch and the water bottle in the other hand I slung my bag on my shoulder and made my way to the basketball court as I did not want to get stuck and trampled upon in the corridors. The push and pull were quite a roller coaster. And I bet hundred rupees that I would end up with a swollen shoulder or a dislocated one with the way things were proceeding. I bumped into at least thirty people and almost fell on a few as I covered a distance of thirty feet. The herd of us children ended as quickly as it had started and later travel from the quadrangle to the basketball court as quickly as the breeze.

As the next turn, I had to take to reach the court was right, I shifted towards the right of the corridor. Yet, as soon as I was about to turn, I bumped into someone. And surprisingly enough, that person fell! How that happened is still a mystery of sorts to me. That guy had messy brown hair and quite a fair complexion with blue eyes. Though I apologized and offered him to stand up according to common courtesy. He was not that mad and forgave me right away. Which had something cany about it. Not only that, but he was also good at continuing the conversation by asking how my exam went? what was my name? which class I was in? and some of my likes and dislikes. All the while smiling brightly and creating a friendly atmosphere that I forgot my mother's warning to be wary of strangers. Before I knew it, we shared basic information about each other. Though more of mine than him. James, was it? Well, next time I better be careful about sharing things with a total stranger. He was quite good at extracting information after which I found myself scolding myself on the inside. That even the cute ones and most friendly ones can be dangerous.

After that, I continued straight, and Wala! I reached the basketball court. Now the hard part had started. You might want to know why. Well, after the exam, I and my friends decided to meet at the basketball court, henceforth now I had to pinpoint where they were. The line of the canteen was right next to the court. So, it was like half the court was where people were trying to stand as if at the edge of a cliff desperately clinging onto one another while the rest of the court was comparatively deserted. The decision was an easy one. I was not going to fling myself into the other side of the court which was crowded just to locate my friends. It was just too troublesome, and I loved my convenience more. Fifteen minutes, fifteen whole minutes which felt like hours was spent in locating those girls as I did not wish to mingle inside the crowd of people shorter than me as well as taller, in any way it did not benefit me in any manner at all.

The line leading to the canteen was a mess. Sometimes someone would step on someone else's shoes or an accidental kick and trays containing food backflipping and landing on a passerby's head followed by a roar of laughter. I waited on one of the elevated seats which overlooked the whole court near the back gate which for some reason was blocked and turned into a parking lot for students to park their bicycles.

Usually, it was used as a place for our house photos and a place from where we shot heightened people would go to try and spot our respective teachers carrying the class registers during the fire drills. Then what else was left to do? Once I spotted my friends, I called out to one of them and waved my hand to signal where I was located. And the lateral group followed along as we finally regathered and started bombarding each other on how the paper went and expected marks. Only these points in our conversation were honestly relevant and had a serious atmosphere after which we switched the topic to our upcoming plans for the vacations as if we knew what was to happen with excited anticipation. Just don't question the duality of being drained to fully energetic in a matter of seconds. At one point it became a norm in our group.

The homecooked lunch which was packed in the morning started to look too little to satisfy our needs. So, when we decided to mix all our lunch boxes it was bliss. The food which seemed to be less turned out to be a feast as Sara, who was confused as to what she wanted to eat from the canteen bought three platters. It was as if, in the middle of the desert I found an oasis and drank water as if it were a precious jewel from which I would never tire.

Truth be told, normally mom won't allow me to eat from the canteen. But since it was the last exam of my ninth grade, I somehow managed to convince her. Yet, I did not spend a single rupee of what was given since the shared lunch was more than enough for us. Some was even left even though we ate a lot. The final day before the vacation had filled everyone with mixed feelings. Laziness since the people just ended the exams, enthusiasm for the upcoming holidays, and sadness for those who were to leave due to their parents being posted out of the station. And of course! happiness as we had a lot of fun chatting away on relevant or non-relevant topics.

Before I knew it, it was time for the school gates to open soon after which I would throw away all my books and scream the dialogue of the queen of hearts "off with their heads!". The thought itself was quite satisfactory. After which I would laze around like anything until it was time to join back as a tenth grader.

Me and the entourage decided to go towards the school gate and bid our farewell there and so we started our voyage with chitter chattering. But, as we were about to leave the court, I saw my class teacher who was announcing on the microphone that all

students from class nine A were to gather in our original classroom located on the second floor of the school building. For some time, I was in confusion as to why our class teacher would request us to assemble in our classroom. Curiosity got the best out of me!! as I started to want to go to the classroom to find out what was the mysterious announcement about Among my friend group Sara too was in the same class as me. Bidding farewell with dramatic hugs with those who were not in the same class as us we parted ways as if it was the last time, I would ever see them.

As we went to the nearest staircase to reach the second floor and for what seemed like the two hundredth time, I wished that we were allowed to use the lift which was right next to the staircase. But it was only for those who had a disability or were school staff members. Hence, climbing the staircase was inevitable. Huffing and puffing, not from tiredness but from a sour mood we reached the classroom. I think I was the twentieth person to enter the classroom from among the forty-four students. The rest of my classmates came in not that long after me.

The backseat of the first row was my favorite seat in the class. Not only was it like a cozy corner, but it was also a window seat through which we could see the side garden with its beautiful flowers. But the curious chatter of my fellow classmates was quite amusing where we divided everyone into groups and came up with various reasons for why the teacher called us here. Not that I was active or passive, but I did enjoy speculating. Still, three people were missing from the whole group along with the teacher which was quite a curious scene as it was none other than the teacher, who asked us to assemble here. So, when we all were arguing about things that we did not know will happen or not, there was a sense of mutual agreement that something was up, and it was like an unsaid universal truth.

So, after another five minutes, latecomers finally arrived. It also brought about another uproar along with it. The dress code for the exam was our summer uniform which was a white shirt with the school logo on the left and a blue skirt with a lot of folds. And for those, who still felt cold, black legging and as for the hair accessories, we were allowed to wear whatever we wanted. But those three were wearing something else. The first one was wearing a black suit. I mean seriously, you are a child? A child! I agree you do look good, but still why? The other two were no less.

One was wearing a pair of jeans and a T-shirt and the other even though was wearing casuals, out of all things chose to wear a night suit!

The first thing which came to my mind was, did our teacher call the whole class to set an example out of those three? Believe me, when I say, I was not the only one with such a thought. Before anyone else could say anything, pin-drop silence fell. As the teacher came to the class and it was quite a scary atmosphere as everyone consciously or unconsciously were holding their breaths and waiting for the verdict to come out. So, there we were forty-one students holding our breaths in silence so that our thumping hearts could be clearly heard and four clueless people not knowing why there was such a heavy atmosphere. Made it quite a sight to be seen. As a third person of course but being involved in it was quite awkward. The first to break the silence was none other than our teacher.

"What's wrong with all of you guys? Aren't you going to wish your classmates on their birthday?" I just knew it, it was detention. Wait, wait, wait... Did ma'am just say birthday? It was their birthday!? There was first confusion, as to if we heard the right thing or not. Then a sigh of relief that we were not in trouble. Followed by a sudden realization. And the four confused people were still confused.

To avoid us being found out, some of us tried to change the subject while the others congratulated the trio. All the while trying to hide their guilt and avoiding eye contact due to the fact that even being friends with them, we forgot their birthday. I am serious, it made the teacher and the trio even more skeptical and left them with a feeling that something was not quite right. You did a marvelous job! But I guess it was just my luck. Was it not?

The one who came to our rescue was the class president. That guy is a miracle worker, I tell you! The type of person who is so reliable that people come to doubt that he is human or not? And the one who usually takes the blame for others in any situation, thus gaining the full support of the class. Sometimes of respect, we would even refer to him as "Dad of the class". As soon as he took charge of the situation a few dialogues were shared with the teacher as well as the trio. Though I did not pay attention to what was being said. As I was scavenging through my backpack to give something to the birthday people. All I could find were three cupcakes and a toffee each.

To smoothen the whole situation, I interrupted their conversation midway and felt the eyes of the whole class shift their focus on me. This drenched me in a cold sweat I tell you. Yet, strangely enough, my voice did not waiver for which I was thankful, as I placed the three cupcakes I had saved and congratulated them a Happy birthday.

Taking this as an opportunity, the president encouraged the whole class to sing the birthday song. Crisis avoided successfully! The mood after that turned into a happy one as everyone started to move on from the previous yet recent incident. The ability of a human to adapt to a situation is seriously not to be looked down upon.

When I reached my seat again, I could see Sara with a thumbs up. And upon reaching closer heard her say, Good Job Girl! "I did not know you had it in you". To be frank, I really did not know why I intervened in the situation myself. But I guess I did it without even realizing it. Man! The exhaustion from completing the exam was really messing with my head. I had enough of today. It was really making me do strange things and then ending up in a situation like, how did I even get here? While the mingling was happening along with the crowding of the birthday trio, I started to relax a little bit. While glancing out the window, I was just seeing a butterfly fluttering from one flower to another when I felt a slight pat on my shoulder only to turn to find out it was the class president.

"Thanks for helping me just now," he said. I mean seriously, just how much of a good guy can he be. While everyone else moved on from the incident, he still thanked my awkward intervention. "Anytime, glad I could help" really, was that what I just said? Gosh! I was at my wit's end. Wasn't I? Afterwards we did share a casual conversation where Sara too chipped in. And surprisingly enough he was quite an interesting character. And not once did I want to end the conversation.

The class teacher struck the table with a chalkboard duster three times asking for our attention. Once again, the room was filled with silence. It wasn't because we were scared or anything, but really liked our class teacher and appreciated all that she had done for us during the past year. And so, another speech began. "Guys, I know you all are having fun. And this is the last day that you will be in class ninth. First of all, congratulations for passing and your promotion to the tenth standard". A round of applause did follow this dialogue. But what I found the most interesting was when a group of people also hooted. Though who they were was not found out, rather acknowledged, and not rebutted. Which was more of a surprise since the teacher usually did not like such behavior and gave punishment for the same and was quite strict about it as well. Yet, she just continued. "I also know how hard each one of you has worked hence I prepared a little something for all of you". This sentence started a curious murmur among us students.

As ma'am went near the door and came back with a box in hand. "Gautham, as the class president, would you like to distribute the gifts I prepared?" The ever-so-reliable guy did exactly what was asked of him. A pouch was distributed each of different colors and everyone could tell that something was inside as well. The twinkling eyes of the teacher waiting with anticipation as to whether we liked what she prepared was quite obvious and if I say so myself was all the encouragement, I needed to open the pouch. What I saw inside was quite touching. Not only were we gifted with a pouch each, but there was also a pen, sticky notes, whitener, pencil, eraser, and all that could be required as a stationary set in the pouch. The detailed manner in which all the pouches were arranged differently made it quite clear just how much effort was put into each. Showing how much we meant to ma'am. I really could not stop that smile from appearing on my face back then. A fond memory that I will try to retain.

As a topping on the cake, the birthday trio too began to distribute gifts for which we all were called in the first place, for. By the end of it all, I had won a magnificent pouch in my favorite color blue. A packet of small heart-shaped candies 25 each, 5 lollypops, and a v7 pen I fought with my sister to obtain, were given as a gift. I was actually glad I was carrying my usual school bag that day or else, I would have been playing a juggler's ball. Judging by the fact that I also had my science books, notebooks, lunch box, water bottle, and a pencil box with a clipboard to be carried as well.

Being a student who did not use the school bus or van meant that it was my own duty to go back home safe and sound. Since my house was just a fifteen-minute walk away, it was quite easy to go back on my own. Being dismissed after all of that seemed quite strange since the loud chatter of everyone seemed to have ended as quickly as it had started. And now the peaceful stroll through the park behind the school which was a typical route to return home was a bonus for me.

The Park was owned by the government and maintained voluntarily by a retired government officer who looked after the park using his private funds. Having served in the army he had traveled a lot and witnessed many cultures as well as sceneries which led to an open mind and acceptance of different practices. Being from a military and trader family myself, I guess I could understand and relate to his sentiments. Though I took my time on the stroll was because of the way the wonderful flowers of different colors were arranged all around and along with the structure of the pathway and landscape never seemed to bore me.

There I was contemplating as to whether I should check the question paper or not, as I could not revise the paper. Hence led to thoughts such as if I did not do well on the paper the weightage of the final exam was the greatest. So, if it brings my overall percentage then I would have a lot of issues and struggles to receive the high achiever award. I guess it would be better to mark the questions I had doubted and see the approximate marks I would score and if it was good, well then great I was saved. If not, there is no use crying over spilled milk, is there? After a deep breath in and a deep breadth out, I opened the third zip from

the front and took up my science books and the clipboard which had the question paper attached to it. The flipping of the pages as I evaluated the questions as the examiner themselves was quite an awkward situation for some time, specifically the first ten seconds. But later, as I fit into the role quite smoothly it became easier. As I reached the final question which I was quite curious about I found out that I had actually done it correctly. Finally, by the end of it all, I was pleased with my performance. If everything evaluated was correct, then I would score more than fifty-six out of my sixty-mark question paper. Feeling absolutely at ease now, I started to pack my bag with satisfaction, stood up from the bench, and joyfully skipped back home humming my favorite melodies.

I might have forgotten to mention that the pouch, given to all of us contained a notice which was none other than a picnic notice attached with a permission slip stating that students collectively would be attending a picnic near the school itself free of cost if they wished to. I suppose that story is for another time as by the time I had ended this tale it is already night-time, and my mother is calling for dinner. Fret not, for we will meet again. Before I leave, I will give you a glimpse of the picnic which occurred today in form of a poem.

# Humming of life!!!

I see fields as they bloom,

Different beings like butterflies on them loom.

The dashing wind blows across,

Adding to the scenery off course.

The sight I see is quite dreamy,

As I enjoy myself voluntarily.

Stay a bit more can I not?

My previous fugitive I had forgot.

Lost in the moment I say,

But now I must be on my way.

Time and tide wait for none,

Friend or foe it can be both or one.

With my friends, I laugh and dance,

As we see the passersby in a trance.

This life of fire of my younger days,

On remembering still with happiness, I sway.

# 2

# The Lingering Child

It was a day of token which described your long journey in the school. A word which made you remember and associate with all your friends. A prize that cannot be measured as you step into your college day.

# The Lingering Child

It was a usual day with the sun rising and the birds going about their day. Yet, for me, there was a gloomy atmosphere as I held the warm cup of milk and stood near the balcony rails overlooking the park to the left of which a white and green building stood that was familiar to me in many aspects. I could not look at it as I did not have the heart to do so.

Finished with my milk, I let out a sigh and went back inside without looking at the building though I tried to steal glances yet found that something was stopping me and that is how my day seemed to begin. In the bedroom, I marched up leaving the empty cup on the dining table, and went to freshen up. Once done, I came out with a towel wrapped around myself and walked towards the closet, and took out the uniform that I would be wearing for the last time.

Truthfully speaking, I used to have a lot of complaints about it as the plates of the skirt were hard to press and I would usually have to staple safety pins here and there as the height was fine, but the waist size was just so large that if I wore the waist size which would fit me, knee-length would not be met. The shirt was fine, but the black bellies were a headache. Going about the day up and down the school floors to get to respective classes on top of which I would get seven shoe bites every day. Seven, I tell you, Oh! I should call it belly bite, right? The amount of discomfort was one more aspect to be seen.

I still had the hanger in my hand though five minutes had already gone by, thoughts such as "Will I ever wear it again?" roamed my head with nostalgia. Ironic, isn't it? The uniform I wanted so bad to get rid of grew on me and I could not bear to do so and there you have it. I checked myself in the mirror once again after dressing up for the day and proceeded to the dining area as per my daily routine. Today's breakfast was pasta as it was the special occasion being celebrated. What was it? you may ask. Well, it was none other than my last day in the school after which I would graduate to become a college fresher. That young child who entered the school gates at the tender age of four was about to step out of it. Time passes by so quickly sometimes right! Though on exam days it feels like forever.

The celebratory mood I did not want to spoil, thereby I went along with it. Was it just me or did the white sauce pasta, I would usually like to eat taste a bit bland today? Never mind, let's quickly finish as I was going to be late if I did not pick up the pace soon.

So, the hustle-bustle started yet again, yours truly shouting from the table to ask where the water bottle was kept, receiving a sluggish answer from my lazy sibling, that it was near the bedside table. Then the not-so-required jog to get the water bottle just to empty it to fill fresh water inside closed the bottle and tossed it in the open bag lying on the couch as I started to scavenge for the white socks. The aim was off the mark and the water bottle landed on the floor with a thud, hopefully, it did not break as I stood frozen in my tracks near the kitchen door and turned my head slowly with a wide grin to my left where my mom was still eating her share of pasta and received a derisively gaze.

Well, I am screwed, the next ten minutes was lecture time after which I went near the couch and placed the bottle back in the bag with a few dry snacks such as nuts, and almonds mixed with sunflower seeds. I then rushed out of the front door and started my venture down the staircase. I live on the third floor of the apartment building, so it was easy to go down the stairs instead of waiting for the lift every now and then. Reaching the ground floor, I went past the generator and parking lot area to reach the back gate where before even reaching the gate the guard opened the gate so that I could pass by. Such a VIP treatment right, Are you jealous? Moving on, I passed the service lane to find the stray dog blocking my path to enter the park which was my preferred route to go to school. Alright, do not fret it's just a dog. You can do it! come-on and so I went a bit closer and waved my hand in front of me to shoo away the dog. But, in return, I received a taunting expression saying, "is this the best you can do?" and another gaze that clearly said, "weird person". Ahh!!

Two critical hits I lost and then I decided to go through another route, but it seemed like an uncle also wanted to go to the park and after a stamp, the dog went back inside the park. I gained entry to the park. But seriously!! Was a stamp being all that was required? Life is so unfair, forget about my rumbling and let's go back to the main story.

Shall we?

So, I walked upon the uneven pavement till I reached an open gym where there was a split in the pathway towards the left side and after a few minutes of walk a gate towards the right side from which you turn left then right, then a forward march after which the school gate would be found on the right-hand side. Too many rights, right? Not much was out of the ordinary until my group of friends whom I was waiting for appeared in different outfits such as a frock, suit, jeans with tank tops, and strangely enough a tracksuit. Why? You may ask. Well, we were allowed to wear casuals.

Next, we made our way to the basketball court which for some reason was decorated by our juniors as an amphitheater and before I knew it, I was half dragged, half pushed to one of the seats and besieged by my friends in all directions you can name north, south, east, west, northeast, southwest, etc. You can imagine, right?

So, the hasting of the farewell from our juniors began with music, then dance, musical skit, live painting of the school logo, speeches, self-compositions, and last but not the least, testimonials of our juniors who wished us the best for what we could do and to share the profound impact we all had on them. More than a third of the people there had tear-struck faces. Not due to sadness but happiness as we remembered our days running in the corridors to get to class on time just to get scolded because we ran in the corridors. The debate competition we prepared with our juniors to win in the interschool competition and what not! Overall, it was a spectacular display, and the care with which our juniors prepared the whole program was satisfying and great and all the positive words you could ever think of. But most of all, it was pride and happiness that reached their height on the emotional chart. The program of six hours which felt only like a few minutes. But it all came to an end, still, I did not want to leave yet, just a little more I wanted to stay.

I asked for permission to loiter around a bit as the afterparty would begin in another hour or so. Hence, I went to the quadrangle from where I turned and went towards my fourth-grade classroom. My school was divided into two buildings, one was from nursery to third and another was from fourth grade to twelfth grade. Memories of my first day in fourth grade entered and played in my mind.

How I was excited to enter the senior building, how I was imitated by the seniors due to their height thinking that they were huge giants. Yet, the teachers were quite amiable in my eyes as they tried to make sure that we were comfortable. Then fifth grade, where I found out about the western music room and ventured there, the sixth grade where I had to say goodbye to some of my friends as we chose different languages. Then seventh grade, I really enjoyed the library as a sanctuary from the noisy class during the break time and the 3D lab a new way for me to find interest in studies as it was no longer theory but practical implementation. Then tenth grade where I performed science experiments and many more.

I gazed out of the window sitting on the table as I had a smile on my face replaying those memories.
To replenish my energy for the after-party that teachers had put together. I took out that box of nuts I had prepared in advance and began munching still in the classroom after which I made my way towards the mini auditorium. The teachers were just about to start as I reached the third floor of the building and entered the auditorium only to be led to my allotted seat with the help of my friends who had already made a group. Some standing on the chairs for what reason you ask. Good question, I still myself don't know why.

Moving on, we again sat there and listened to around five more speeches. In between as a breather, a skit and three dances were performed. But I was surprised to see my old Hindi teacher who taught me in fourth class, since I saw ma'am be a strict teacher dance, well consider me colored in surprise. We, students, were then called to the stage one at a time while the refreshments were being served alongside and upon calling of our names, we made our way towards the stage to receive a badge with one quality of ours written such as Akshat was Mr. Diligent. Yet, there were few titles that brought about a few crackles here and there, like Sumit Mr. Troublemaker.

Not to mention that when my name was called, it was right after I put a piece of chocolate cake in my mouth, and I did my best to swallow it up as I made my way to the stage and almost choked on a small piece as I thanked ma'am for the badge stating me to be Miss studious and my friends were enjoying the spectacle, as they knew that I was not what was mentioned on the badge rather the opposite thereby enjoying the irony. Well, all in all, the day turned into late evening as we were dispersed. I stood at the gate as I remembered the nickname grandmother gave me "lingering child" I guess that was true. I am a lingering child. I ask, are you too?

# The Lingering Child

If you look too far into the past

You might forget about the road ahead

The growth is slow, yet fall is so fast

Time seems less to put your faults to bed

In this comfort of the past, I want to rest

I know I must move on, yet I linger still

The trails crossed the peace is best

Time waits for non, so stay you will till?

The sand of the hourglass falls

Each tiny particle till the end

Get up I say to you for duty calls

The broken heart time will mend

The heart will break

But despair not for the broken live on

To let go is a decision you must make

Say goodbye tough to pieces you are torn

The first step is the hardest

Yet the following are bearable

A diamond heart is the strongest

But I guess to possess, that I am not able

Walk on, walk on you must

A glass half full a glass half empty

While either way, it is enough to quench the thirst

Move you must, for this is your new reality.

On the bare tree a life sprout

Hope is still there, wait for a little

No goodbyes, one wishes to shout

No matter what! There is no doubt.

9 798887 044156

Printed by Libri Plureos GmbH in Hamburg,
Germany